This book
belongs to

....

Other books by Mick Inkpen

ONE BEAR AT BEDTIME

THE BLUE BALLOON

THREADBEAR

KIPPER'S TOYBOX

KIPPER'S BIRTHDAY

KIPPER'S BOOK OF COLOURS

KIPPER'S BOOK OF COUNTING

KIPPER'S BOOK OF OPPOSITES

KIPPER'S BOOK OF WEATHER

PENGUIN SMALL

LULLABYHULLABALLOO!

British Library Cataloguing in Publication data

Inkpen, Mick
Kipper.
I. Title
823.914 [J]

ISBN 0-340-56564-0

Text and illustrations copyright © Mick Inkpen 1991

First published 1991 by Hodder Children's Books
Paperback edition first published 1992
12   11   10   9   8   7

Published by Hodder Children's Books,
a division of Hodder Headline plc,
338 Euston Road, London NW1 3BH

Printed in Italy by L.E.G.O., Vicenza

Kipper

Mick Inkpen

Hodder
Children's
Books

a division of Hodder Headline plc

Kipper was in the mood for tidying his basket.

'You are falling apart!' he said to his rabbit.

'You are chewed and you are soggy!' he said to his ball and his bone.

'And you are DISGUSTING!' he said to his smelly old blanket.

Out they went.
'That's better!' said Kipper.

But it was not better. Now his basket was uncomfortable.

He twisted and he turned. He wiggled and he wriggled. But it was no good. He could not get comfortable.

'Silly basket!' said Kipper…

…and went outside.

Outside there were two ducks.
They looked very comfortable
standing on one leg.

'That's what I should do!' said
Kipper. But he wasn't very good.
He could only…

...wobble.

Some wrens had made a nest inside a flowerpot. It looked very cosy.

'I should sleep in one of those!' said Kipper. But Kipper would not fit inside a flowerpot.

He was much too big!

The squirrels had made their nest
out of sticks.

'I will build myself a stick nest!'
said Kipper. But Kipper's nest was
not very good. He could only find…

...three sticks!

The sheep looked very happy
just sitting in the grass.
No, that was no good either.
The grass was much too...

...tickly!

The frog had found a sunny place
in the middle of the pond.
He was sitting on a lily pad.
    'I wonder if I could do that,'
said Kipper.

But he couldn't!

'Perhaps a nice dark hole
would be good,' thought Kipper.
'The rabbits seem to like them.'

But it was not a rabbit hole!

Kipper rushed indoors and hid underneath his blanket.

His

    lovely

        old

           smelly

                blanket!

Kipper put the blanket back in
his basket. He found his rabbit.
        'Sorry Rabbit,' he said.
He found his bone and his ball.
        'I like my basket just the way it is,'
yawned Kipper. He climbed in and
pulled the blanket over his head.
        'It is the best basket in
the whole, wide…

. . .sssssssssssshh

hhhhhhh!